My Real Name Is Princess

written by Jay Dale

illustrated by Mélanie Florian

All the children sat on the floor.

"Good morning," said the new teacher.

"My name is Mrs Kay.

What's your name?"

"My name is Bill," said a big boy
with red hair.

"My name is Lee," said a little girl
in a spotty dress.

"And what's your name?" asked Mrs Kay,
looking at the little girl at the back
of the room.

"My name is Princess," said the little girl.

"Oh, no, my dear," smiled Mrs Kay kindly. "What's your **real** name?"

"My real name **is** Princess," said Princess.

"What a beautiful name!" smiled Mrs Kay.

"Do you feel like a princess?"

"Sometimes," said Princess sadly.

The children sat at their desks
and began their work for the day.
Some children listened to stories
while others read books with Mrs Kay.

Some children got their books and pencils,
and began a story.

Princess got her book, too.

Her story was all about a little girl
who loved to dance.

Princess worked very hard all morning
and she didn't rush at all.

She loved to make up stories.

They made her feel happy.

After lunch, Mrs Kay told
the children to sit down.
Then she disappeared into her office
and came back with a blue box.

"I have a surprise for you," she said,
and slowly opened the box.
Inside was some soft green paper.
Mrs Kay unfolded the paper
and took out a pretty red cape.
The cape had beautiful silver
and gold stars all over it.

"Ohhhhhh!" said the children.
"Who does that cape belong to?"

"Well," said Mrs Kay,
"this is my special star cape.
I like to give it to someone
who has been working very hard.
They can have it for one week.
They can even take it home!
It's a very special cape and, sometimes,"
said Mrs Kay to the class,
"I think it's a little bit magic!"

"Can I put it on?" shouted Ted
from the back of the room.

"No!" said Dara. "I want to put it on!"

11

Mrs Kay asked everyone to stop and listen.

"There is one child who has been working very hard all morning," said Mrs Kay.

"Who is it?" shouted Tom.

"Well," said Mrs Kay, "it's Princess.
Her story is very special
and she has tried her best today."

Mrs Kay stood up and took the star cape
over to Princess.
She placed it carefully around
her shoulders and did up the ribbon.

Princess smiled happily.
She felt beautiful.

All the children clapped and clapped.

Mrs Kay smiled at Princess.

"Do you feel like a princess?" she asked.

"Yes!" said Princess. "I do!"